Amazonas

This special signed edition
is limited to 1000 copies.

Amazonas

Alan Peter Ryan

Amazonas

Alan Peter Ryan

CEMETERY DANCE PUBLICATIONS

Baltimore
❖ 2012 ❖

FIRST EDITION
ISBN-10: 1-58767-233-2
ISBN-13: 978-1-58767-233-0
Cemetery Dance Publications Edition 2012

Cemetery Dance Publications
132-B Industry Lane, Unit 7
Forest Hill, MD 21050
Email: info@cemeterydance.com
www.cemeterydance.com

DEDICATION

for Bob Booth

1

The river, the river. She thought it would never end.

Day after day, as the long, narrow boat labored painfully upstream through the unpredictable current near the shore, she sat on a rough wooden crate on the deck and tried to read. The sheet of filthy canvas, precariously suspended on slender poles above her head and only erected after she asked for it, provided a bit of shade, but the small shady patch shifted with every turn of the boat in the water. From the unceasing heat and suffocating humidity and ferocious insects of the Amazon forest there was no escape at all.

The days ran together and she was no longer certain of the calendar, the date, the day of the week. Days of savage heat and humidity and blinding sun and the glare from the river itself. Days and nights of insects beyond one's ability to marvel at their size and variety, their countless numbers, their insatiable hunger. Mornings of clammy, sticky fog. Afternoons of sudden violent rain that pounded flesh and soaked clothing, food, everything. Nights of frogs, millions of frogs, whose endless and deafening chorus of croaking made shallow and unrefreshing even the most exhausted sleep. How long had she worn the same sweat-soaked, yellowing clothes?

And the river itself. It flowed indifferently beneath the narrow *batelão*, pushing it this way and that, snagging it on hidden twisted roots and sunken tree trunks, jarring it suddenly and dangerously against submerged rocks. The Indian crew kept the boat near the shore because the current was slower there, but the same obstacles that slowed the current threatened at every second to overturn the boat.

Edwin was in a terrible state, barely sleeping at night, muttering aloud to himself during the day, and screaming at the six straining Indians until he was red in the face. In the first days after they left Manaos and started upstream, she had thought he was doing this to impress Crown with his energy and determination. Now she was not so certain. Now she suspected that the heat or some growing illness or simply the power of his obsession was affecting Edwin's mind.

For weeks now, they had barely spoken. And Crown rarely spoke at all.

Henrietta sat for hours with her head tilted forward above her book, shifting her position only to try to stay in the meager shade. But she was not reading. She was watching Edwin. She watched him chew at his fingernails and spit into the river. She watched a vein in his temple that never stopped throbbing and the tic that made a muscle twitch beside his eye. He had taken a particular dislike, for no visible reason, to one of the Indians in particular and she watched him cuff the man in the head more than once.

One time when he did it, she saw the Indian slowly slide his brown fingers down to the long knife at his belt that he used for slashing at roots that held back the boat. Edwin had turned away and didn't see him. After a moment, as Henrietta watched, the Indian subsided and left the knife where it was, but she was certain that, if Edwin continued as he was, he would murder her husband one day as soon as he had the chance.

The thought made her catch her breath. And the most frightening part of that thought was not the fear of losing her husband. She had passed beyond fearing that. But if she did lose Edwin, here, so far upstream from the last outpost of civilization, surrounded by the green-walled forest and the dark and tangled terrors it contained, what in the name of God would become of her?

Most of all, she feared Crown.

Edwin's drunken whispering about something he called "the slave tree," that last night in Manaos when he'd had too much to drink and told her they were going even farther upriver in the morning, was disturbing and frightening too, but not as frightening as this man Crown.

He was the immediate threat, she was certain of that.

A big man, wide shouldered, broad-chested, always slick with sweat, but indifferent to the heat, the rain, and the stinging and biting insects, Crown rarely spoke aloud. Watching him day after day, Henrietta thought she would hardly recognize his voice if he did speak. He said nothing, even when the leader of the Indian crew, who seemed to be the pilot, consulted with him. Whenever the river divided, or when one of the side streams called *igarapés* appeared in the bank, the Indian would turn to Crown, seated always atop the little wooden hut but near the prow of the *batelão*. And

Crown would nod, or point this way or that, and the Indian would execute his order. That silence was inhuman, unnatural. Henrietta's flesh crawled whenever she looked up at his broad, silent back.

And the look of him. The size of him, the dirty blond hair carelessly chopped short, the pale blue eyes that never stopped moving in his expressionless face, the thin and bloodless lips. And the face itself lumpy with knotted muscles, tense and tight and often pulsing with energy that he now kept rigidly contained but that might one day, she was certain, explode in sudden violence.

And somehow, with the whispered sharing of some secret of which he was in possession, or with some outlandish promise, or with an offer of some rewarding opportunity, this man Crown had taken control of poor Edwin's mind and so brought the two of them, Edwin and her, onto this straining, creaking *batelão*, up the slowly narrowing path of this unknown river, and into the heart of the forest.

Poor Edwin. She had stood by him for more than four years now, encouraged and aided him as best she could in all his failed schemes in Boston, in New York, in Baltimore, in Washington, in Richmond. She had even responded hopefully when he had come crashing into their boardinghouse room one day, rattling on at length that South America was the new land of opportunity and Brazil the fastest road to a fortune. Henrietta cared nothing about fortunes, but she cared about her husband. And when he'd used a third of the money that still remained to buy passage to Rio de Janeiro, she'd smiled and pretended to share his high hopes and enthusiasm.

No more. Now she feared that he was mad.

She passed hours on the *batelão* sorting through her memories of the places they'd been and the things they'd seen and struggling to find something good in it all. With difficulty, she found only two things she could think of as good.

One was the exotic sights of the tropics. First, bustling Rio de Janeiro, a lively little city on a beautiful bay. Then, after Edwin learned there that the real money was on the Amazon River and they had to retrace their route back up the coast, past the picturesque towns of Salvador, Recife, Fortaleza, to be immersed at long last in the colors and smells and the stunning heat of Belém at the mouth of the

Amazon. Then there was the terribly slow boat up the river to Santarém, and after that an even slower boat farther up the river to Manaos. Never had she expected, in this Year of Our Lord 1906, to be looking at such sights in the middle of a jungle: the teeming docks and crowded streets, the elegant men and women and their fine carriages and clothing, the mansions big as palaces, the handsome British Customs House, and the new, British-built Floating Dock that was the talk of all the town. And the beautiful Opera House, its lovely pink marble glowing softly in the blazing sunlight. And the churches, the beautiful old baroque churches. Edwin, of course, did not want her to go out alone in Manaos, and a few people in the streets did look curiously at her, but nonetheless she had ventured out to explore a little. In the relatively cool darkness of a small church across from the Opera House, the Igreja de São Sebastião, she had slipped in through a side door she found open and spent several afternoons in that quiet haven, praying fervently that Edwin would come to his senses and that this terrible journey would end. Not all these memories were happy ones, but Henrietta prayed that in time the pain would fade away and leave only the exotic sights in her mind.

That was one of the good things, the store of extraordinary scenes she would remember all her life.

The other was that Edwin's obsession and his conviction that he was moving rapidly closer to his chance at a fortune had come to fill all his thoughts, leaving room for nothing else. Since they had left Belém on that first riverboat, he had not turned to her at night, had not even touched her. She was grateful for that, and she thought often in these recent weeks above Manaos that if he reached for her ever again, even once, she would be sick to her stomach.

The *batelão* was in a clear patch of water now, only twenty feet or so from the bank of the river. There was no need for the Indians to get into the water and swim ahead against the current and then haul the boat with ropes past rock after rock, or to use the long poles with hooks at the end to pull it laboriously forward by overhead branches, walking up the length of the narrow deck along the length of the pole each time. Here the bottom of the river seemed to be clear and solid enough and the

Indians were standing, three on each side of the boat, using the other poles with the forked, crutch-like base to push it ahead.

Suddenly, without warning, the bow struck something unseen beneath the water.

The boat shuddered along its whole length and instantly began to slip sideways in the current. The six Indians, who were barefoot on the deck, kept their balance and, leaning hard on the poles, managed to keep the *batelão* from turning broadside to the current and being swamped, but Edwin lost his footing on the wet deck and tumbled with a curse into the river. His head emerged almost at once, his long hair streaming across his face. Sputtering and coughing, spitting water, he swore loudly at the Indians as he quickly scrambled back onto the boat, and again when he stood, dripping, on the deck.

When the boat struck, as it had done so many times before, Henrietta's book had slipped from her limp fingers to the filthy deck. Once Edwin was safely back on board, she bent forward with a sigh to pick it up. The paper cover and some of the pages were bent and wet and soiled from the muddy deck. She spread the book open on the crate beside her, in the sun, to dry.

Crown, sitting cross-legged atop the tiny wooden structure at the front of the boat, thick arms braced at either side, never moved or spoke.

Mercifully, the water remained calm for a while after that and the boat glided smoothly around another of the endless curves in its winding route through the forest.

At such places, along the quiet stretches, during the first weeks of travel from Manaos, Henrietta had sometimes turned to look back down the river, measuring the distance they had come from civilization, but now she no longer did so. Looking back only made vividly painful to her how far they had traveled into the trackless unknown. The river was always the same, always stretching farther ahead, and every passing day convinced her even more strongly that it would never, never end.

2

At nights, camped among huge granite boulders or on a rough slab of rock beside the river, if they were lucky enough to find one just before darkness overcame them, her restless sleep was disturbed by dreams, and through the dreams swirled Edwin's red face, Crown's indifferent eyes, the hand of an Indian slashing with a knife. Always the river foamed threateningly around her. Insects darted through the dreams, puncturing her skin, invading her eyes and nose and mouth and ears, leaving stinging, itching welts on her neck, her arms, her hands. Animals, all of them dark and shapeless and nameless, snorted and grunted and pawed and rustled the leafy branches around her and above her. Monkeys chattered and pointed and laughed at her predicament. Lying stiff and aching on the rough rock, half asleep, half awake, she couldn't tell if the beasts were real and threatening or if she had imagined them. She lay there, muscles knotted, fingers trembling, eyes squeezed tightly shut, afraid to move.

And always in the dreams there was a tree, some kind of tree she had never seen before, and Edwin's breathless voice and slurred words filled the dreams, repeating over and again his excited report in their airless little room that last night in Manaos, but now its sense was all twisted. Or was it? What exactly had he said that night? Did it make sense then? Did it make sense now?

"A slave tree," he had said again and again. "A slave tree! Don't you see? Don't you understand? That's what Crown called it. A slave tree! We can have our own. All we want. Grow them. Thousands. Millions. As many as we want. Don't you see? Don't you see? A slave tree!"

Bewildered, frightened, watching his bloodshot eyes and smelling the liquor on his breath as he paced the tiny room, she had said at first only, "Slaves? A tree? I don't understand, Edwin."

He had raised his arms then and she saw that his fists were clenched. For a moment, she thought he was going to strike her, to pound the sense of what he was saying into her. But he had only flailed his arms around in frustration, lost his balance, and bumped heavily against the shabby and scarred dresser that was the only furniture in the room other than the sagging bed on which she sat.

"A slave tree, for God's sake!" Edwin roared. And again, bringing his mouth and the smell of the liquor suddenly close to her face, his voice lowered to a harsh whisper, "A slave tree. It grows slaves. All you want. All you have to do is...is...harvest them, for God's sake. Pick them like goddamn fruit." And, his voice rising again and ringing in the shabby little room, "Slaves, Henrietta, goddamn it, don't be so thick, you understand English, don't you?"

She stared wide-eyed, her head moving slowly from side to side.

Edwin dropped suddenly and heavily to the edge of the bed beside her. At once, she turned her face away from the rank, sour smell of him. And prayed that he would pass out.

"Look at me!" he snapped. "Listen to me!" He made a drunken effort to calm himself and lowered his voice again. "Fortune. A fortune. This will be our fortune. Don't you see? We'll go home rich."

"How, Edwin?" she breathed. "How?'

As he opened his mouth to answer, he choked on phlegm in his throat and she thought he was going to be sick right there in the tiny room and she closed her eyes, but he only coughed and quickly recovered.

"Sell them," he said, still short of breath and wheezing. "We'll sell them."

"Sell them, Edwin..." She could not stop shaking her head. "Edwin, how can you think of such a thing? Are you talking about human beings? And slavery is gone. Gone for forty years at home. And twenty here in Brazil, I think."

Edwin braced his hands against the bed behind him and leaned back.

Henrietta used all her will to force herself to turn and face him, to study his eyes and his expression.

Edwin grinned at her.

"Crown," he said.

Henrietta continued shaking her head.

"Crown," Edwin said again, still grinning. "Crown can sell them." He nodded to emphasize his reassurance to her. "He knows how. He knows the right people. Believe me. He knows how."

Edwin's eyes closed for a few seconds and he slipped lower onto the bed. Then he stirred, shifted his position to his side, and reclined on one elbow. Henrietta had to turn on the bed in order to watch his face.

"Who is Crown?" she asked.

"My partner. I met him today. We're partners. He has...has this tree, the slave tree. Upriver. In the jungle. He's the only one who knows. And me. I know. Because I'm his partner."

"Edwin, where did you meet this man?"

"Today, I told you. Today."

Edwin's eyes were closing. His head sank sideways, closer to the bed.

"Who is he?"

"He has a...place...upriver. A long way. Tomorrow."

"What? What did you say?"

"Tomorrow. We're leaving tomorrow. Pack up everything. We're leaving in the morning. With Crown."

Upriver! Even farther up the river!

"Edwin!"

His eyes were closed, his cheek resting on his outstretched arm. Saliva ran from the corner of his mouth.

"Edwin!"

"A slave tree," Edwin mumbled. He settled his face on his arm. "Grows slaves," he mumbled. "All you want. Goddamn slaves."

"Edwin?" she whispered.

He didn't stir, only breathed heavily.

"Edwin?"

And suddenly he rose up from the bed, red-rimmed eyes blazing into hers, saliva wet on his chin, sour breath reeking of drink, and stabbed one finger with its ragged, bitten fingernail close at her face.

"And you listen! You listen to me! Crown has the slave tree. He knows where it is. Nobody else. Do you see? I need him. I need him! Later it'll be different. But now I need him. Whatever he says, we do. Whatever he says. Do you understand? He tells you something, you do it. Whatever he says. You! Whatever he says. You do it! You do it!"

And so, waking or dreaming, she feared Crown more than anything else.

3

The river narrowed.

Or was it still the river?

Sometimes the water seemed as smooth and tranquil as a lake, its glassy surface rippled only by insects and feeding fish. A few times they came to short stretches of rapids where the water foamed loudly, and she and Edwin and Crown got out of the boat and climbed up the slippery rocks alongside the river while the Indians, shouting and gasping for air, used the ropes to haul the *batelão* upward against the rushing current.

Sometimes, when the river divided and then, an hour or a day later, became one again, Henrietta thought they must have passed an island. But she didn't think much about it, or about anything else. There was no way of knowing for sure. There was no way of knowing anything for sure.

She saw that Edwin was losing weight, or perhaps the exercise was making him more fit. She didn't know.

She was losing weight herself. Her clothing was loose on her now and she could see the stretching tendons and jutting knuckles in her hands. They were old hands for a woman of thirty. She compelled herself to swallow the food prepared by one of the Indians, the bitter, muddy liquid Edwin said was coffee, the sticky mass of farina made from yellowish manioc flour, the rice with evil black things in it that she had learned to pick out and push aside indifferently, the half-raw fish the Indians caught in the river and wrapped in waxy leaves and roasted over a fire, the strangely shaped fruits they sometimes found near the river that had at first given her terrible stomach pains but now gave her nothing, not even nourishment, she thought.

Edwin wrote in his leatherbound journal nearly every day. He would come to the stern of the narrow boat and crawl into the *toldo*, the barrel-roofed, thatch-covered structure that stretched for more than half the length of the *batelão* and was the only shelter it offered, other than the tiny wooden hut near the prow which was Crown's exclusive preserve. Henrietta watched him do this, and to the extent that she thought about anything, she thought he was keeping this activity a secret from Crown. When she began noticing that he made a mark in the book each day, as soon as he could after they came aboard in the morning, she realized that he was counting the days and making notes, or trying to, on their route through the forest, the trackless forest that looked the same everywhere. She watched him do it. He would hide in the cramped *toldo* and scribble hurriedly in the journal. He kept the book in the one battered suitcase that was all that remained to them now, that contained all their earthly possessions. He kept the stubby pencil with which he wrote in the pocket of his stained and torn pants.

The suitcase was also where Henrietta kept the precious paperbound books that she had bought in Rio de Janeiro. She remembered the day she saw them in one of the market stalls in, what was it called, Largo do Paço? In the center of the city. She had no Brazilian currency and Edwin kept trying to hurry her along, but she had picked up the books, pulled a single American dollar bill from her purse, and handed it to the vendor, a dark-skinned man, she recalled, who had only two teeth in his mouth. He had scrutinized the bill carefully, turned it over and studied the other side while she waited anxiously, and finally stuffed it into a pocket, and she had taken Edwin's arm and walked away quickly with her prize before he changed his mind.

She had read all five of the books on the coastal steamer from Rio to Belém and on the riverboats, and she would read them again but she could not. Not now. They were books about civilized places written by civilized men. What did Tuscany or the Lakes District or the Auvergne have to do with her? Now she could only hold one of them in her hands day after day, where it served merely as a fragile talisman, now stained and filthy and torn, of her former life.

Crown remained silent. He kept a barrel of the fiery cane liquor called *cachaça* always within his sight and beside him when he slept, which he did with a loaded pistol in his hand and his other guns and the supply of ammunition beneath him, indifferent to discomfort. Every night, after they had camped and eaten the evening meal, he doled out a small gourdful of *cachaça* to each of the Indians, who carried their gourds a little distance away to sit in a circle and drink the liquor by themselves. A few times, after a hard struggle to drive the *batelão* against foaming rapids, and once after they spent most of a day unloading all the cargo and carrying it up a steep incline and then hauling the empty boat after it and then loading it again, he had poured out an extra serving for the exhausted Indians. But not even then did he speak.

Guided by silent nods from Crown, the Indians steered the *batelão* into ever narrower streams.

One day, Henrietta suddenly realized that, while she was dreaming or dozing, the *batelão* had glided into the forest itself. The river, if river it still was, had widened and spread out, flooding a low-lying area. She looked around. The harsh sunlight was gone, leaving only a kind of twilight beneath the green canopy high above. The Indians, silent now, used their long poles to push the boat quietly along past the thick trunks of trees. There was nothing in sight that could be called land, only the trees rising up straight from the water. For a long bewildering moment, it seemed to Henrietta that the boat was floating among the stately dark columns of a cathedral.

The rough columns sprouted flowers that clung to their sides. Once, as they glided close to a thick tree trunk, Edwin stood at the side of the boat, braced himself as the boat slowly slid past it, and plucked from the trunk of the tree a large, handsome flower. The whole plant came away from the tree intact, a thick bed of dark green leaves perhaps as much as eighteen or twenty inches in width, and the open flower itself at the center of it, some kind of orchid, white and pale violet, seven or eight inches across.

Edwin made his way back along the edge of the boat. He stood in front of her and, smiling, handed the flower to Henrietta.

She took it from him and smiled in return, as best she could. She examined the plant, the fleshy dark leaves, the broad but delicate flower, the root structure that had clung to the trunk of the tree. She sniffed the flower and rubbed the large petals between her fingers, again and again and again, realizing with a start that brought a lump to her throat that she had touched nothing so soft in...how long?

The plant was interesting, the flower beautiful, its perfume faint but sweet, and she welcomed the feel of it in her rough hands. But after a short while, all she could think was that now, torn from the trunk that gave it life and nourishment, the flower would die.

She held it a little longer, caressed its soft petals a little longer, and then, leaning over to the edge of the boat, dropped it gently into the dark water. Perhaps the water would help to delay its death.

The plant floated upright, bobbing a little from the movement of the boat, and then drifted backward as the boat left it behind.

Henrietta did not look back.

4

And another day through the forest.

At night, the Indians lashed the *batelão* to
a tree and they slept in the cramped *toldo* and
on the crowded deck as best they could and ate
only a little of the fruit they carried.

And another day.

And on yet another day, as Henrietta sat as
always on her crate at the stern, one hand holding her unread book, the other listlessly sweep-
ing insects away from her face, the *batelão* grat-
ed against something soft and yielding, tipped
upward a little at the prow, and came to a stop.

The Indians dropped over the sides into
the water and shoved the *batelão* forward as far
as they could.

Henrietta opened her eyes wide, forced
herself to focus on the scene.

They were still in the middle of the forest,
still in the dappled twilight, still surrounded in
every direction by the tall, straight tree trunks
that rose so high above. But here, she saw, the
floor of the forest must have sloped upward
ahead of them, upward and above the level of
the still water, and the boat had run aground.

Ahead of them she saw dry land, the forest floor itself.

She forced herself to stand. She gripped the edge of the thatch-covered *toldo* and pulled herself upright.

Yes, dry land. Muddy near the edge of the water but dry beyond. Dry land as far ahead as she could see in the dim forest light.

The Indians were already unloading the boat.

Edwin made his way back to her, then helped her along the narrow deck at the side, up to the prow, and then jumped down to the mud and helped her down beside him.

The mud was slippery, but she made her way through it by herself until she stood on solid ground. There was little undergrowth here, not enough to block her view, and now that she stood on it, she could see the very gradual but definite upward slope of the forest floor.

Edwin came up beside her, leaned close to her, put his mouth near her ear.

"We're almost there," he whispered. "Almost there."

5

They walked for several hours through the forest. Crown led the way. Henrietta could not imagine how he followed a specific route among the numberless identical trees.

The Indians, bent, straining, grunting, sometimes slipping to the ground, carried all the gear and cargo from the boat. Edwin sweated beneath a heavy load, even Crown bore his share, and Henrietta carried the suitcase and a coil of heavy rope, as much as she could manage.

Above their heads, birds and monkeys clicked and coughed and chattered and shrieked. The canopy overhead was dense and admitted only a little diffused light to the forest. The lack of sunlight prevented anything but the trees from growing, and so the walking itself was relatively easy.

Full darkness came suddenly. Just as Henrietta realized they were in the very last of the light, Crown dropped the load he was carrying to the ground and the rest of them instantly did the same. They made a camp quickly, and a fire and a meal, ate quickly, and bedded down as best they could.

Just as her eyes closed, Henrietta noticed that three of the Indians were not lying down. Instead, they seated themselves with their backs to each other, like stacked rifles. They drew their knees up and wrapped their arms around their legs. Their eyes were wide open, and those of the Indians facing the dying fire glittered in the light.

What were they watching for? What were they guarding against?

At least now they were sleeping on dry ground, away from the sound of the rushing river, and she was thankful for that. But what danger threatened the camp? What danger in the forest required watchmen to guard them?

But what did it matter?

She closed her eyes and slept.

Moments later, or so it seemed, Edwin shook her shoulder to wake her. He had a mug of the bitter, grainy coffee for her. The fire had been refreshed. One of the Indians was preparing manioc mush.

By the time they'd eaten, the darkness had brightened to the half-light of day. They began walking again, weighed down by the gear.

They walked most of the day.

After many hours, Henrietta slowly became aware of a bright light ahead, a clearing, a bright, sunny clearing in the forest.

She saw a house in the clearing. A white-painted house, the paint flaking in the brutal sun. A European-style house, with two floors and windows on every side and a wide, shady verandah across the front.

She thought she was dreaming.

Behind her, one of the straining Indians murmured something to another.

Edwin's raspy breathing drew closer to her.

"The *estância*," he whispered. "We're here."

He struggled ahead of her with his heavy load in order to walk beside Crown.

Stumbling, Henrietta followed as best she could and at last, amazed and blinking at the sudden brightness, emerged into the clearing and the sunlight. Without stopping, she dropped the suitcase and the ropes and stumbled across the clearing toward the house.

So this was the object of their long journey, this old *estância*, the land presumably cleared and the house built by someone who thought to harvest rubber or nuts or other slow treasures from the forest, then later abandoned, then found and commandeered by Crown.

Wearily, Henrietta mounted the four solid wooden steps to the verandah. The double front doors of the house stood open. She saw furniture inside. Her eyes rejoiced in the shapes and angles of familiar objects.

On the verandah, in the deep shade, pushed carelessly away from the door, were six wooden rocking chairs. They were soiled with dirt and rain and bird and animal droppings, but Henrietta didn't care. Knees trembling, she walked unsteadily to the nearest of them, tested its solidity, and sank into it.

The chair was real. The house was real. Everything around her was real, and Henrietta wondered only if this place she had come to at last was heaven or hell.

6

"The slave tree," Edwin said. "I want to find it before Crown comes back."

Crown had spent that first night, and then another full day and night, at the house. He had eaten, slept, eaten, and then slept more, in one of the rooms upstairs, keeping the door closed, saying not a word within Henrietta's hearing, and then he had left them and gone into the forest alone. He would be back, Edwin thought, in a week or ten days. Edwin did not know where he had gone.

They had better food now. The Indians had time to hunt in the forest and they brought back meat, some kind of pig, and Henrietta had taken a large, ragged chunk of the thing for herself and Edwin.

After a long night's sleep, stretched across what had once been a fine bed, she had explored the house. There were candles and kerosene lamps and kerosene to light the darkness. There was a kitchen of sorts attached to the back of the house. She used most of her strength in cleaning it and clearing away encroaching green growths, but she found pans and pots and bowls and a clay oven. And in the open space beyond the kitchen one of the Indians showed her the remains of a vegetable garden and a thickly luxuriant banana tree bearing ripe fruit. And when she gestured and made sounds and conveyed to the Indian the idea of water, he led her a short distance into the forest and there, like a miracle, was a narrow stream.

That night, they ate roast pork and rice that she cleaned before cooking it and some sort of tuber from the garden that she boiled until it was tender and bananas that she fried, lovely sweet bananas, in a little of the pork fat. And she drank a mouthful of *cachaça* herself after the meal.

She brought three big bowls of food out to the Indians who waited just beyond the verandah. They took the food and carried it away and ate it without a word but, later, one of them, the leader and river pilot, came and stood silently at the bottom of the steps before the doorway until Henrietta noticed him, and only then did he turn away and walk off. She understood at once that he was thanking her.

Later that night, they were all sick from the unaccustomed food and the quantity of it but, even as Henrietta doubled over outside the rear door of the house, gagging, she looked forward to another meal of the same.

Days passed.

Adequate food. Hours and hours of deep and dreamless sleep. Clean clothing and her own body washed quickly in the little stream. A roof above her head. A room. A bed. Doors that could be closed. Purposeful labor that produced a visible result. So quickly that it surprised her, her thin and weakened body began to recover, her mind began to grow clear, and her thoughts fell into orderly patterns.

She and Edwin flourished in those first few days alone at the house without Crown, and with the Indians outside but invisible, appearing only for meals and to bring more meat. Flourished and grew strong, although they hardly spoke at the beginning.

And when at last he did speak, Edwin said, "The slave tree. I want to find it before Crown comes back."

Henrietta continued with her work and did not reply.

Edwin paced on the verandah.

It was their sixth day at the house. When she had opened the suitcase to examine their clothing, she had found another short pencil and she kept it secret from Edwin. Each morning now, she used it to make a mark inside the cover of one of her books. She was counting the days.

It was on that sixth day, the day he spoke Crown's name aloud to her and mentioned the slave tree and paced up and down outside, that Edwin's illness first appeared. By nightfall, he had already passed through two cycles of shivering and teeth-chattering chills and then rank, sweat-soaked fevers and he was ranting in wild delirium about his childhood.

Malaria.

Henrietta knew it was malaria. She had heard about it and perhaps she had read about its terrors in *Harper's Magazine* or in that book by Mary Kingsley or somewhere else. She knew it was malaria and she knew at once that Edwin was going to die.

7

Two days later, Edwin awoke weakened but clear-headed, apparently free of symptoms. He insisted on getting out of bed, over Henrietta's protests, and he was able to eat a little. Later in the morning, he was able to lean on her shoulder and walk to the stream, where she washed the acrid sweat from his body.

All the while, she wondered how long it would be before he spoke of the slave tree again. And how long it would be until the chills and the fevers returned. And how long it would be until he died.

About midday, as they sat together in the shade of the verandah, half-dozing in the heat, Crown came walking out of the forest and crossed the clearing to the house. Eight small, dark-skinned Indians, their faces painted red and purplish blue, walked behind him.

Edwin stood up, a little unsteadily, to greet Crown. As Crown climbed the steps to the verandah, his gaze passed briefly across the two of them, then returned to Edwin's pale face and came to rest there. He studied Edwin intently, in silence. Edwin asked about his trip. Did everything work out all right? Did he have any problems? Did he get what he needed? All of it nonsense. All three of them were aware that Edwin knew little enough of Crown's business and nothing at all of what he'd been doing this week or more. Except that he had obviously recruited new Indians.

Crown's pale blue eyes flicked from Edwin's face to Henrietta's and met her gaze directly.

It was the only time since she had first laid eyes on him in Manaos that she and Crown had communicated in any way. And she saw instantly, in those two or three seconds, that Crown had recognized Edwin's condition and knew the same thing she knew.

She was surprised at first that his gaze met hers and spoke to her so clearly, if silently, but by the time the big man moved away and passed on into the house, she had grown alarmed at that long and lingering look.

8

The next day, everything seemed very different, largely because, after he'd eaten a big meal that Henrietta prepared and then slept for eleven hours, Crown appeared transformed.

And he talked.

He spoke slowly at first, as if he were just growing accustomed once again to human speech and then finding that he could manage it. He was back now, Henrietta saw, in his natural environment, like one of the beasts of the forest. He was at home, not expansive but obviously comfortable. Obviously in charge. He dominated everyone around him by his simple size and presence and by his instinctively assumed authority, and he knew it. He could survive here and, in his own way, prosper. And, of course, he could help other people to survive, or he could hinder them. In Manaos and, in a sense, even when traveling on the river, he had been in the civilized world, a world of interlocked needs and obligations and rituals. Here, in the forest, at the *estância*, Crown ruled all, possessed all, including the slave tree and the Indians, and needed nothing more.

Except for Edwin. Edwin, whom Crown had sought and found in the civilized world and brought back to his own world. Although his need for Edwin was not yet clear.

The day after his long sleep, Crown wiped his mouth clean with the back of his hand and sat back, rolling his shoulders.

"Tomorrow," he said, "I'll take you to the slave tree."

Henrietta wasn't sure if she was to be included, but she wanted Crown to know that she was going with them. She took a breath to steady her voice.

"How long will we be gone?" she asked him. "Will we need food?"

"We won't need food," Crown said. And again his eyes lingered on her face.

"It's nearby, then?"

"Near enough. You'll see."

Edwin leaned forward and Henrietta saw at once that her husband was straining to appear businesslike.

"I've been thinking about this," he said, "about the business side of it, I mean. Of course, I haven't seen the tree yet, but..."

"You'll see it tomorrow," Crown said.

"Well, you see, Crown, I've been thinking that we'll need boats..."

"Not yet."

"I see. Not yet," Edwin said. "But don't you think we'd be better off if we..."

"We don't need boats yet." Crown's tone closed the subject. He leaned forward against the table. "Anyway, there's a problem."

"What sort of problem?" Edwin asked.

Crown shook his head, briefly, little more than a flick of his chin.

"Never mind now," he said. "You'll see."

While Edwin sought another gambit to prolong the conversation, Crown looked at him and said, "You told me you know how to use a gun."

"A gun. Yes. Sure. Of course, I'm not a great marksman, I'm really a city boy, but naturally I can use a gun."

Crown turned his head to look at Henrietta.

"You?"

"No." Suddenly her heart was thumping and she couldn't breathe. She lowered her head for a second to conceal the deep breath she had to draw in. "Unless I had to."

Crown watched her, waited for more.

"If I were in danger, I mean. Or Edwin."

Still Crown waited.

"Or you, of course."

And even as the words escaped her lips, she regretted speaking them, regretted thinking them, and she hated Crown for making her say them and hated herself for falling victim to his trick.

For one instant, before she could control herself, she felt her thoughts blazing forth from her eyes as she looked Crown straight in the face.

His expression did not change but he might as well, she saw, be smiling. Instead, he slowly lowered his eyes and let them rest for a moment on her bosom.

Henrietta rose at once from the table and went to light one of the kerosene lamps.

A short while later, lying awake on her bed, fully clothed, and thankful that Edwin had returned to the bed he'd slept in when he was sick, Henrietta wondered what men did in the forest to ease their need for sex. She could not imagine Crown doing what a friend had described to her in whispers fifteen years ago, half her life ago, claiming even to have seen her own brother doing it to himself in the woods. The thought repulsed her. But maybe a man like Crown would do it. With a start, she recalled something she had long put from her mind. Weeks or months before, in a busy market in Belém, she had surreptitiously watched, equally horrified and fascinated, as a small, fierce-eyed monkey, oblivious to the cage he sat in and any eyes that might observe him, did that very same thing.

9

Early in the morning, after a hasty breakfast of coffee, fruit, and manioc, Crown assembled the two groups of Indians in the clearing in front of the house.

Watching the scene, and listening intently, Henrietta gathered that the Indians belonged to different tribes and spoke different languages, although she saw no signs of animosity between them. Crown, it appeared, spoke at least a few words of each language.

Interpreting his gestures as best she could, Henrietta understood that Crown told the new Indians, the eight he had brought back a couple of days before, to remain near the house and clearing. She thought he told them to hunt for meat. And she was certain that he issued them a warning. He was carrying a long green stalk he'd sliced from a plant. As he spoke, he split the outer green layer with his thumbnail, peeled it back, and tossed it away. Then he put the pointed end of the white core into the corner of his mouth and gnawed at it while he kept his gaze fixed on the Indians. Finally, he bit through the core, tossed away the long part, and spat the ragged, chewed lump that was left in his mouth onto the dry ground at the feet of the leader. Without another word, he turned away.

Then he led the other Indians, the six who had brought the *batelão* up the river, to the side of the house where, Henrietta knew, a wooden lean-to, dried gray and warped by the sun, held a rusted and rotting collection of tools. After several minutes, the group returned and waited silently for further instructions in front of the verandah. Each of the Indians was carrying a shovel. They shifted their bare feet uneasily in the reddish dust of the clearing but not one of them said a word.

Crown briefly surveyed the two groups of Indians standing there in the sun and they seemed to shrink a little as his cold gaze passed across them. Then he turned to Edwin and Henrietta, waiting in the shade of the verandah.

And he grinned. He actually grinned.

"Come on, then," he said. "Let's go. I'll show you the slave tree."

10

They left the clearing of the *estância* at the opposite side from where they'd first arrived from the river. There was no path, no trail, but Crown walked with confidence through the half-light. Deeper and deeper they penetrated the forest.

Crown gestured to the Indians and made them spread out and walk side by side, in line with him, as close together as the trees permitted. Henrietta thought it was because he wanted to keep an eye on them.

When they'd been walking for a long while, perhaps two hours, Henrietta guessed, one of the Indians on her right, one of those who had come up the river, suddenly stopped, gasped, and spun around, his eyes rolling. The others halted at once, crouched, tensed, looked at the one who had turned, searched the forest ahead, then behind and all around them.

Crown instantly raised his hand, holding his pistol, his finger at the trigger. Arm stretched out straight, he aimed the gun at the head of the Indian who had made the noise. The Indian was only about eight feet away from him.

Edwin and Henrietta were startled by the commotion. They at once searched the forest in every direction but there seemed to be nothing out of the ordinary. In the stillness, five large parrots, flashes of emerald green and golden yellow and blazing crimson, rose together from a branch above them and flew low among the trees directly across their line of sight, the sound of their flapping wings receding quickly in the distance.

Crown spoke a few words to the Indian. Who was nearly shivering now with fright.

When Henrietta looked directly at the man, she realized he was the one Edwin had struck several times and who she had been certain was going to kill him. Now, trembling with inexplicable fear, he looked incapable of killing anyone.

Crown repeated what he'd said, his voice low, insistent, commanding. The Indian's eyes wavered and searched the forest, then came to rest on the barrel of Crown's gun for several long seconds. Then, very slowly, he turned—forced himself to turn—back in the direction they'd been walking. And at last took an uncertain step forward. And another.

They continued, but now Crown dropped back behind the line so that he could see all of the Indians as they moved slowly through the forest. He kept the pistol in his right hand and he unslung the rifle from his shoulder and carried that in his left. Still another holster and gun hung at his left hip.

He carried a straw bag, slung from a rope across his shoulder and chest, that rested against his broad back. Looking at it now, and its heavy, uneven shape, Henrietta realized that it contained more guns. She did not doubt that they were already loaded.

Hardly knowing where she found the courage, she hastened her own pace and fell in step beside Crown. Edwin paid no attention to her move and just kept slogging forward.

"What happened?" Henrietta asked Crown.

She was surprised when he answered at once and his voice sounded quite natural. Often, when they were on the river, she had wondered how this stony-faced, silent man had talked to Edwin and, in a single day or perhaps in only a few hours, persuaded him to join this mysterious and difficult venture. She had barely exchanged a few words with him herself but now she found that Crown could speak reasonably. Or at least that he could seem to.

"That one," he said, "is supposed to be a wise man in his tribe. Some kind of chief or medicine man. Knows things the others don't." He kept his voice low, as always, but he answered without hesitation. "The wise men in each tribe know the places in the forest where people should never go. Bad places. Dangerous places. Places where evil spirits live."

Henrietta continued walking, keeping her eyes down, watching where she placed her feet. The forest was thicker here and sometimes now they had to hold a thin branch aside from their faces as they passed.

"That's how I found the slave tree. I made some Indians take me to all the bad places they knew. All the places that belong to evil spirits."

"The slave tree"—Henrietta was surprised to hear her own voice actually saying the words aloud—"belongs to evil spirits?"

"You make up your own mind," Crown said, lowering his voice even further. "You're a lot smarter than your husband, anyway. I know you are."

Before Henrietta could reply, she suddenly realized that the forest ended not far ahead of them. They were coming to a large clearing or a river, she knew, because now she could see dazzling beams of sunshine ahead and the forest had become thick as a jungle where brilliant rays of light penetrated the canopy above.

Crown, without stopping, raised his right arm and pointed with the gun.

"There it is," he said.

Henrietta's eyes searched ahead of them but the clearing was apparently encircled by a ring of thick undergrowth that admitted light but blocked her view.

"There," Crown said. "There it is. The slave tree."

She could hear the suppressed excitement in his voice. But now, even as he moved forward, Crown's eyes roved from side to side. He was watching the Indians.

They stepped out of the forest, the two white men and the woman and the wide-eyed, staring Indians. They came to a halt in the blinding sunlight at the edge of an immense clear area.

At the center of the circular clearing, rising dark and thick and tall above their heads, its lowest branches no more than fifteen feet above the ground and spreading straight and wide from the thick trunk, stood the slave tree.

11

"Wait!" Crown said. His voice had a sharpness in it that Henrietta had not heard before.

Using the gun to emphasize his directions as he gave orders, he quickly rounded up the six Indians into a tight group. With a few words more, he gave further instructions. The Indians nervously shuffled into a line a few feet apart from each other and, as Crown pointed with the gun, began digging with the shovels they'd carried from the *estância*.

Crown moved around to face the Indians as they dug into the earth so that, if any of them looked up from their work, they immediately saw him and the gun.

This was done very quickly. As soon as the work was in progress, Crown looked past the laboring Indians at Edwin and Henrietta, whose attention was divided between the huge tree in front of them and Crown and the Indians.

He lifted the rifle in his left hand and pointed with it to the tree.

"Go ahead," he told them. "Have a look."

Walking slowly, side by side, Edwin and Henrietta moved forward, across the wide ring of bright sunlight and into the broad circle of darkness beneath the tree.

The tree dominated the clearing. Nothing else could grow in the dark circle of shade cast by its dense foliage. The ground beneath it, within the circle of shade, was littered with dead, dry growth that had dropped from the tree, but was otherwise clear. Nothing green grew there. Once she was beneath the tree, Henrietta looked back and all around the clearing. It was almost perfectly circular, and the area without vegetation extended beyond the shadow of the tree, so that the clearing, surrounded by dense green forest, was ringed by a circle of sunshine thirty or forty feet in width. Forest plants should have thrived in that sunlight but, instead, the sun shone down on dry, lifeless dirt. As if, Henrietta thought, nothing else could grow or would grow or wished to grow anywhere near this tree itself.

The trunk of the tree was nearly six feet in diameter and rose straight from the ground. It did not appear to taper but rose massive and thick, like a column. There was no sign of roots at its base, as if the structure that gave it support and nourishment were far beneath the surface, buried deep within the earth. This was unusual because trees in the Amazon typically have shallow roots, visible on the surface of the ground. This column of wood, rising straight and regular to its lowest branches, appeared to be made of a tight and knotted tangle of thick wooden strands, like heavy cables or tendons pulled and twisted so taut and intertwined that they adhered together and formed one solid mass. Its surface was golden brown, smooth, free of any bark, and even seemed to gleam a little. And despite the deep creases and crevices that stretched and curved vertically up the length of the trunk, it was—unlike all the trees Henrietta had observed in the forest, in both dry regions and those that were flooded—free of any orchids or any other flowers or growths adhering to its surface. And, though the dark foliage overhead made it hard to be certain, she thought there were no birds in it, either.

She reached out and laid a hand on the twisted surface of the trunk. It felt warm.

She craned her neck and looked up into the thick, green darkness overhead.

The lowest branches, perhaps a dozen or fifteen feet above her head, grew long and straight at right angles to the trunk, dividing and subdividing again and again. The dark green leaves were thick and fleshy—perhaps, Henrietta thought, like the leaves of a succulent plant, some sort of giant succulent whose tough, fibrous texture could gather and hold a considerable quantity of water.

As her eyes adjusted to the shade after the bright sunlight beyond and she began to see details, Henrietta made out other, larger shapes within the foliage. She saw pods. Wherever a branch divided, at the point of division one or two or three pods hung downward on long woody stems. These pods were dark green like the tree's leaves, and appeared to be sturdy and firm like the pods that contain ordinary green peas. Indeed, they were about the same shape, thick and flattish and long, but a foot or two wide at the middle of their length and tapered at the lower end. They varied in size, probably according to their stage of growth. The largest of them appeared to be five or six feet in length.

No. No, Henrietta thought. Crown is mad. And Edwin is mad. Such things cannot be.

Edwin squeezed her elbow and she jumped.

"Look!" he whispered. "Look!"

His head was turned upward, his wide eyes turned upward, his mouth open in wonder.

"Look!"

Henrietta disengaged her arm from his grip and moved away, circling around to the far side of the tree.

Her feet kicked up some of the dried vegetation that had dropped from the tree, a carpet of shriveled leaves, here and there a branch, mostly dried but one still relatively fresh, and the remains of many large pods that had fallen, some dried so that they crumbled when her foot brushed against them, a few others fresher, still retaining some of their shape but without their fullness as they decayed and sank in on themselves and became part of the earth.

She looked up from examining the ground. Edwin was off to her right, still staring up into the tree, his mouth still open. At the far side of the tree and the clearing, in the blazing sunshine where they had emerged from the forest, Crown still stood above the Indians and the Indians were still digging in the soft earth.

Crown had divided them into two groups of three, facing each other. The soil yielded readily to the shovels and the Indians had already dug a sizable trench. As she watched, Crown gave them an order and five of the Indians stepped down into the trench and dug even faster, tossing shovelfuls of dirt up and out onto the level ground. The sixth, who was the same one who had cried out on the way to the clearing, the wise man of his tribe, seemed to offer some protest, said something to Crown, something challenging or defiant or perhaps merely fearful. Crown spoke once more and raised the gun in his hand and pointed it at the Indian's stomach. The Indian stared back at him, his muscles knotted and body tense, but after a few seconds he lowered his head. His lean dark body seemed to shrink inward and he stepped down into the trench beside the others and resumed digging.

Henrietta approached the trunk of the tree again, touched it again with the tips of her fingers, ran them along one of the twisted strands of wood. It still felt warm.

What was happening? What was Crown doing? Were they waiting for something?

Edwin was walking around slowly beneath the tree, kicking at the dead vegetation that littered the ground.

Henrietta turned from the tree and walked toward the far side of the clearing, farther away from Crown. She stopped at the edge of the shade cast by the tree but kept her back to the trunk of it and to Edwin and Crown and the Indians.

She felt clear-headed and numb, deadened, both at the same time.

She felt that she should pray but she no longer knew how, no longer knew what she believed or where help might be sought.

She forced herself to focus on the green wall of forest in the bright sunshine before her. In order to keep her mind functioning, she tried to see it not as a wall but as separate plants. She wondered how far the forest stretched in this direction.

She closed her eyes. Opened her eyes. She had no power to change her situation. No power to save herself. Edwin was sick. The malaria was going to return. Edwin was going to die. There was no way out of the forest. She would be dependent on Crown. Despite the presence of the tree behind her and above her, it was Crown who filled her thoughts.

Directly behind her, a few feet away, something crashed through the leaves and branches above and thudded heavily to the ground.

She spun around with a cry.

It was a pod.

A large, heavy pod had dropped to the ground not ten feet behind her.

She stared at it. And, after a moment, remembered to breathe. The falling pod could have killed her if she'd been standing beneath it.

She looked up. The tree was perfectly still, as if nothing had moved.

Her heart pounded in her chest. She tried to catch her breath.

She took a step forward.

She saw Edwin moving quickly toward the pod.

Across the clearing, Crown raised the hand that held the rifle and yelled, "Wait! Don't touch it!"

The Indians had stopped digging and were looking in the direction of the pod. Facing Henrietta. Eyes wide.

They were standing in the trench they were digging. They were waist-deep in it. Henrietta vaguely wondered how long she'd been daydreaming.

Crown yelled something at the Indians.

Three of them slowly lowered their shovels to the ground but they continued looking toward the pod.

The three others stood as if transfixed. Then one of them, the wise man, suddenly spun around toward Crown and hurled his shovel at the white man. But he lost his footing for a second as he turned in the trench and the heavy shovel landed on the ground near Crown's feet.

In the same instant, Crown crouched low, raised his arm, and fired the pistol directly at the man's face from five feet away. The bullet shattered the Indian's head in an explosion of red spray. In the same instant, the man's arms flew up straight above his head and his body crumpled backward into the trench.

A swarming cloud of large birds, flashing yellow and red in the sun, erupted from the forest all around, screeching in sudden terror, wide wings flapping heavily, and disappeared into the depths of the forest.

Monkeys shrieked and chattered high above and green branches all around shook and rustled at their frantic flight.

The slave tree, sheltering no birds or monkeys, remained still and silent.

Crown fired five more times in rapid succession, aiming each shot directly at one of the Indians, and they dropped, heads snapping back and arms flailing, across each other in the trench they themselves had dug.

Crown still held the rifle in his left hand. He laid it carefully on the ground behind him, then stood up straight. He dropped the pistol into the holster on his right hip and stood a moment, flexing his hand. Then quickly he re-loaded the gun.

He stepped toward the edge of the trench, bent over and retrieved one, then another, and then another of the shovels. As he pulled each one out of the trench, he tossed it aside. He had to move along the trench to reach the others. He found one, tossed it on the ground with the rest. He found another and stepped down onto the pile of bodies to free it. As it came away in his hand, a piercing scream cut through the air. He tossed the shovel down. He searched for the last one. The scream stopped for a second, then began again. Crown found the shovel, used the toe of his boot to roll the body aside, and pulled it free. The scream stopped again, then resumed. Crown began shoveling dirt into the trench from the heaps all around its edge. While he worked, the screaming continued until, finally, with a sound of gagging and choking, it stopped and silence once again filled the forest.

12

Silence.

Finally, breathing. Her own. A sound more like strangled wheezing than human breath.

Henrietta had willed her eyes closed but could not close them.

She watched Crown across the width of the clearing. His figure was bright in the sun. He was using the toe of his boot to move and then tamp down into the fresh dirt a hand and forearm, dark and lifeless, that projected from the newly formed mound where the trench had been.

Despite the constant moisture in the hot air, Henrietta felt her lips and her open mouth grow dry.

She had never before seen a human being die, let alone six men shot to death in front of her eyes.

Crown finished his task, threw the shovel aside, and straightened up.

Henrietta turned toward Edwin.

He wasn't there.

Then she saw him. He was lying on the ground, on the litter of dried vegetation from the slave tree. His knees were drawn up to his chest and his arms wrapped tightly around himself. He was facing her and she could see that his eyes were wild, his teeth chattering madly, his body shivering violently.

Crown was walking toward her, his feet kicking aside the dead leaves and bits of branch and the rotting pods. When he passed the trunk of the tree and noticed Edwin off to his left, he changed direction and headed toward him.

Henrietta forced herself to move. Her knees were trembling almost too much to support her. She walked slowly to where Edwin lay, shivering and twitching.

She and Crown reached him at the same time. They stood together above him, looking down. Edwin, oblivious, did not look up.

Crown snorted.

"A week," he said. "I give him a week. At most."

He turned and looked her directly in the face.

"That means you're my partner now."

And suddenly his thin lips parted and he smiled at her, revealing remarkably bright, white teeth.

Henrietta took a step backward.

Then, without another glance at Edwin, Crown walked off toward the pod that had fallen from the tree.

"Come here," he called. "I want to show you something."

When she didn't move at once, he called again over his shoulder, *"Come on!"*

13

There was nothing she could do for Edwin. That was obvious. She couldn't even comfort him, ease his pain and fear. He might or might not recover from this spell, but for the time being he was beyond comfort in either case.

She leaned forward and touched his quaking shoulder for a second, then rose and followed Crown. She did not look past the trunk of the tree toward the place where the Indians were buried.

The pod lay on the ground at Crown's feet.

To Henrietta's eyes and her numbed brain, it looked like nothing so much as a gigantic peapod.

"You know what's in this thing," Crown said. He touched it with the toe of his boot. "Your husband told you, didn't he?"

He had, but only after a fashion. To supplement the madness Edwin had described, Henrietta had skimmed through his journal during her few brief clear-headed moments on the river, hiding from both Edwin and Crown beneath the *toldo*. Later, at the house in the forest, she had read it through page by page during Crown's absence and Edwin's illness. She knew what the pod contained.

"He did, didn't he?"

She could hear the sharp edge in Crown's voice.

"Yes," she said. It was more a mere exhalation of breath than a word.

"Look at this," Crown said.

He dropped to his knees beside the pod and drew the knife from his belt.

The pod had a thick stem, two inches across and a foot long. The flat, round end of the stem had separated neatly from the branch where it grew, like any other fruit or pod that matures on the tree or the vine and then breaks free and drops to the ground of its own ripe weight.

A single natural seam ran the length of the pod, from the stem to the tapered point at the other end. Crown inserted the blade of the knife into the seam near the stem end, pushing it in five or six inches, and then drew it slowly the full length of the seam. The pod was nearly six feet long, and tough, and even for Crown this job required some effort. The wide, flat pod, like a clamshell, remained closed while he worked at it.

When he was done, he rose and came around to the other side, where Henrietta stood. She took a step to her side, away from him. Crown knelt again and, using both hands spread wide apart, gripped the cut edge of the pod and jerked it sharply back. The wide flat bottom of the pod, held down by the weight it contained, remained in place, but the top snapped away with the sharp crack of a crisp, fresh vegetable.

Crown stood up and looked at her, watching for her reaction.

Henrietta, breathing hard through her open mouth, stared at the thing on the ground.

The pod contained a human being.

14

A black male human being, perhaps five feet in length, on his back in the flat canoe-like bottom of the open pod, arms lying straight at each side of the body. The skin an intense ebony beneath a thin oily slime of a pale green color that also coated the interior of the pod. The eyes were closed but the lids fluttered faintly as if in sleep. The lips were slightly open and there was a hint of white teeth within. More of the pale green fluid seeped slowly from the nose and mouth. Beneath the oily coating the head was covered with thick fuzzy black hair. The features of the face were Negroid. The limbs were perfectly formed. The palms of the hands and the soles of the feet shaded to a lighter color than the rest of the skin. The sex lay to one side, at rest.

From the interior of the pod where the stem joined it, and apparently an extension of that structure, a flexible vine-like cord snaked across the head and chest and was joined to the body at the belly, where a navel would be.

Henrietta, leaning forward in spite of herself, examined the body as one might that of a newly born infant. Her eyes instinctively sought the marvelous details, the eyelashes, the lips, the ears, the gently curving fingers, the fingernails, the foreskin, the feet and toes.

Her eyes drifted upward to the chest again. She thought she detected a faint flutter of life.

"It's worth a fortune," Crown said.

His voice cut into her mind like a sudden scream. She jumped and a shiver rippled across her shoulders and down her back.

Crown knelt and took hold of the vine-like thing that connected the black body to the pod. With the blade of his knife, he severed it about two inches from the belly. The stump that remained stood out straight from the abdomen and seeped more of the pale green, sap-like fluid.

Crown took hold of the split edge of the pod and rocked it back and forth a couple of times. The figure inside it slid a little each time. Crown heaved forcefully, then jerked up the edge of the pod with a grunt. The body tumbled out, flopped over, and came to rest on the ground. Crown pulled the empty pod aside and pushed it away with his foot.

The face lay with its cheek on the ground, the mouth open now more than it had been. Green sap ran from the corner of the mouth

and from the nose. One arm was caught beneath the body. The other lay limp and twisted
at an unnatural angle. One knee was slightly
bent. The back and shoulders were broad,
the black buttocks round and neatly formed.
The legs were spread a little apart and revealed
more of the pale green fluid seeping from the
anus.

Without speaking again, Crown pushed
the toe of his boot beneath the body, under the
ribcage, and flopped it over once more onto its
back, in the same manner, but less gently, that
one might turn over a newly born calf or lamb
in the straw of a barn.

Dirt and dried leaves and rotted bits of
twigs adhered to the hair and face and body
now, lifted from the ground and held by the
sticky coating.

Henrietta was oblivious to Crown. She felt
a rush within, a sinking and contraction in her
chest, her breasts, her stomach. She fell to her
knees beside the body and, with trembling fingertips, brushed and picked debris away from
the eyes, the nose, the mouth, the cheeks, the
ears.

She wiped her fingers on the hem of her
dress.

Crown stood beside her and watched, then made an impatient sound.

"The damn thing is probably dead already," he said.

She touched a black shoulder. She did not look up.

"I need these things to live." Crown's voice was flat, intense, as if he spoke through clenched teeth. "These things are worth a fortune. We'll collect them, harvest them. And we'll sell them. They'll be worth even more than rubber. Slave labor without slaves. No problem with laws. These things aren't men, they're not human. Cut them open and they're green. They're like bananas or coconuts. But they're different. They can work. And this is the only source of them. I've searched the whole forest. This is the only tree, the only place they grow. And I have it."

Without looking up, Henrietta forced herself to speak.

"What do you mean, it's probably dead already?"

"You'll see," he said, and she heard the instant bitterness in his voice. "But it's up to you now. You figure out what to do."

"Why did you kill the Indians?"

She had not even meant to say that.

"Hah! They knew the way to the *estância*. They knew where the tree is. They're afraid of the place and they don't talk about it, but they knew. I can't take any chances."

She kept her gaze on the black body before her. She touched her fingertips to the chest, but her hand was shaking and she could not be certain if she felt a heartbeat.

"And will you kill me too?"

"I need you. I needed your worthless husband but he's as good as dead. Now I need you. I can't be everywhere, here and in Manaos, at the same time. I need white people. I can't rely on these stinking Indians for anything. I need white people. We'll share the money."

"What makes you think . . ?"

But Crown ignored her. He turned and walked quickly away to the edge of the clearing, into the ring of sunlight. He looked up toward the sun, checked its position, and strode back to stand over her again.

"Get up," he said. We have to start back to the house. I have work to do on the way. We'll be a long time going back, longer than it took coming here."

Henrietta didn't move.

"I suppose you want me to carry your husband back with us."

At last, she raised her head and looked at him. And past him, to where Edwin still lay curled in a tight knot on the ground.

"He's going to die, you know," Crown said. "And soon. You know that."

He shifted his feet, waved a hand at the black body on the ground.

"Just like these damn things. Look at it. It's dying already. They die. They just die."

He pushed the toe of his boot against the body on the ground, then suddenly drove a hard kick into the upper part of the nearest black leg.

The body jerked a little.

"They die!" Crown growled. "Every one of them. They always *die!*"

15

They were a long time making their way through the forest to the *estância*.

Crown carried Edwin slung over his shoulder like a dead animal he'd hunted and killed. Henrietta walked behind him, watching Edwin's head bobbing against the big man's sweat-soaked shirt.

Crown knew the forest and the invisible path between the trees like a creature born within it. He walked purposefully. Easily bearing Edwin's weight and the weight of the rifle and the sack of guns that hung across his back.

He carried a small hatchet in his right hand. Every twelve to fifteen feet, he stopped beside a tree and hacked out a deep triangular wedge. Some of the trees bled a clear or golden sap and twice a thick whitish fluid seeped out from the wood. Crown paid no attention to that. He hacked out the wedge on each and then moved quickly on to the next tree.

Shortly after they started back to the house, as he chopped quickly at a tree, he spoke to her.

"You'll need these," he said. "You'll need to get to the tree by yourself. You'll have work to do here. It's up to you. Think of a way to make those things stay alive."

He said nothing else all the way back to the *estância*.

After that, Henrietta watched more closely and realized that each tree with a wedge was within sight of two others, one on either side. The wedges themselves were in line with Crown's straight path, now made visible, through the forest, so it could be followed from either direction. Each wedge pointed the way to the next.

Birds called loudly through the forest. Once, a family of monkeys shrieked angrily at them from branches high overhead. The only other sound was Crown's hatchet chopping at the trees.

When at last they emerged into the clearing and saw the house, Crown stopped for a moment and slowly scanned the line of trees all around. Then he walked on and, with Henrietta following, stepped up to the verandah, pushed the door open with his foot, and continued inside and up the stairs.

He entered Edwin's sickroom and dumped his limp body on the bed.

"Food," Crown said. "Get something to eat."

Henrietta moved toward Edwin.

"Now," Crown said.

She prepared and fed him something, she hardly knew what.

The day ended and the sudden darkness of the tropics enveloped the house. She lighted lamps. She watched Crown eat.

When he was done, he rose without a word and went to his room and closed the door.

As she moved about, Henrietta, amid her disordered thoughts and resisting the hard knot of panic that threatened to twist her insides, that made her heart race and her breath come short, wondered if the other Indians would return.

But they did not appear. They were gone. Henrietta realized that Crown had known they were gone as soon as he'd reached the clearing.

When she was alone, she went to Edwin. He had not moved on the bed. He was sweating heavily. His lips moved and she heard a low murmur but could understand nothing of what he was mumbling.

She had fetched water from the stream, for cooking, in the last of the rapidly fading daylight, and she tried to get Edwin to swallow some. He would not. Or could not. She lit a candle so she could watch his face. She sat on the edge of the sagging bed, her hand on his arm. In place of physical rest, she tried to empty her mind of all thoughts.

Finally, after she knew not how long, she became aware that Edwin's breathing had steadied and he slept.

She sank down on the bed and slept beside him.

It was full daylight when she woke. Edwin was still sound asleep, his breathing regular. His skin was oily but he seemed not to be sweating.

Stiff and aching from sleeping on her side and in her clothing, she quietly searched the empty house.

Crown's door was open. His guns were gone, all of them, and the sack he used to carry supplies. She went out to the verandah, blinking in the bright light, eyes watering, and looked and listened for a long time.

The Indians were gone.

Crown was gone.

She and Edwin were alone.

16

She forced herself to eat. She gagged on the food at first, but she made herself continue.

While she was cleaning up afterward, fighting the weary weight that dragged at her limbs, she heard Edwin's faint voice calling to her.

She went to him.

She brought him water. It was warm but he drank it thirstily. He told her he felt better. He was weak, but his eyes looked clear and he made sense when he talked. He wanted to go downstairs. He wanted to sit on the verandah.

She helped him down the stairs, supporting his weight, and put him at the table. He slumped forward heavily against it. He would have to stay there. The verandah was too far away.

She brought him more water and he drank it. She brought him manioc mush and fed it to him slowly, a tiny bit at a time, from her fingers, but he had trouble swallowing it and then his stomach weakly rebelled and the mush dribbled from his mouth. He was having a hard time holding his head up.

He fell into a sleep, his cheek resting on his arm on the table, but only briefly.

He raised his head, eyes clear again. He wanted his journal. And his pencil.

She brought them to him.

He reached eagerly but weakly for them. She thought he was unable to focus his eyes.

He needed to write in his journal, he mumbled to her. Needed to keep a record. Record of everything. Details. All important. Be important someday. Pods. Soon.

"Yes," she said. "Of course, Edwin."

He had to write. Soon, the pods...

"Yes," she said, her hand on his shoulder.

He was starting to sweat again. She saw the oily beads of sweat taking shape on his forehead.

"Go ahead," she said. "Write in your journal."

He scrabbled roughly through the pages, his movements uncoordinated. His hands were sweating and his wet fingers left damp stains on the paper. He wrinkled several pages when he had difficulty turning them.

She left him and went out to sit in one of the chairs on the verandah.

She closed her eyes, allowing herself, willing herself, to doze.

After a while, she woke and lifted her face. She sat still for several minutes and studied the clearing in front of the house. The shadows of the trees at the edge of the circle had moved. A couple of hours might have passed. She concentrated on listening, but she heard nothing, only the increasingly familiar sounds of the forest and the occasional calling birds. She wiped her damp face with her hands, and her hands on her dress. At last, she pushed herself out of the chair and went inside.

Edwin was slumped over, his sweat-coated forehead resting on the open pages of the journal.

She stood beside him.

"Edwin? Edwin?"

She took hold of his shoulders and pulled. He was heavy. She pulled again, more forcefully, and brought his shoulders to the back of the chair. His head lolled forward.

She bent over to see his face. His eyes were open, glassy and unseeing. A string of saliva hung from his slack lips. His skin glistened with sweat and, despite the assault of odors in this place, she suddenly smelled the rank, acrid scent of his body and his matted hair. She let go of his shoulders, slowly, to be certain he was balanced on the seat.

The journal, still open on the table, had a large wet stain from the sweat of his forehead across the two pages.

Edwin was dead.

Now she was alone.

17

Two days passed. Or three. Possibly four. She had been strict with herself about making a mark on the cover of her book when she awoke each morning, counting the days in an effort to give order to this existence. But one day she had forgotten, or she thought she had forgotten, and when she later went to put in a new mark for that day, all the little lines on the paper, orderly as they were, seemed meaningless.

She began again, a day or two after Edwin's death. She used the untouched pages at the back of his journal, recording some notation, at least, whenever she thought of it. What she ate. When she hunted for wood to burn. That way, perhaps, she could see the shape of the days and later tell them apart from each other. Even though she knew she would never read what she was writing.

She spent long hours sitting in a chair on the verandah. As she had done on the *batelão* on the river, she held one of the paperbound Tauchnitz Editions in her hand, although she could not focus her mind to read. At one point, reminding herself to make an entry in the journal, she had found the pencil stub and begun writing in the front pages of the book. When she realized it wasn't the journal, she stopped. But then, feeling that the book was more personal, more her own than Edwin's journal, she went on with what she was writing and continued to make her entries there, keeping her handwriting small to make best use of the space.

She wondered how long it would be before she had malaria herself. Or some other disease contracted from the insects, the water, the forest, the air itself. Or an injury that could not be fixed without medical attention. Or how long it would be before Crown reached out for her. Or indeed if Crown would ever return.

She recorded Edwin's death, and how she had buried him, dragging his heavy body outside and down the steps and, after finding a shovel in the lean-to and then searching the clearing for a suitable spot, pulling the body around to the side of the house because there was shade there and she would be a long time digging. When the hole was ready, as deep as she had the strength to make it, she returned to the house and brought out a stained sheet to wrap his body in. But she was too light-headed, too weak, to roll him into it, and she gave up almost at once. She would need her strength instead just to push him into the hole and then cover him with dirt.

She lay on the ground beside his body until she felt she could carry on with the task.

At the last second, even as she pushed at his weight, she suddenly stopped. Doubled over, on her knees, she waited until her breathing slowed. Then she opened the buckle of his leather belt and, with great difficulty, pulled it free from around and under his body.

She gathered her strength once more, tumbled his body into the shallow grave, and finished the job of burying him. By the time she was done filling in the hole, the day was ending and the quick descent of darkness was near.

She stumbled into the house and dragged herself up the stairs to her bed. Ignoring her filthy hands, she pulled off her dress.

She had Edwin's belt with her. Now, before she lay down, she put the belt around her waist and buckled it in place. It hung low on her hips. She would wear it under her dress from now on, so she would always have it with her.

She had read in the newspapers of men hanging themselves with their belts. There was plenty of rope at the house, but somehow a sturdy leather belt seemed to her somehow less brutal, more neat and efficient, more decent.

18

But after she'd slept through the long darkness and on into the bright light of another morning, after she relieved herself and then slowly washed her face and hair and body in the gentle stream, she felt much better. She even felt a little hungry, and no sooner had the thought entered her mind than she felt ravenous.

For two days, she ate and slept, ate and slept and ate again. On the third day, her muscles ached from lack of exercise. She moved things around in the house, the broken bits of furniture and the pots and tin plates she had been using. She washed all of her clothing and what remained of Edwin's. She set aside the worst of it as rags, hesitated over the rest, and finally added the shirts and trousers to her own pile.

She gathered the driest wood she could find from the forest and set it in the sun near the edge of the verandah to dry further. She needed very little for her tiny cooking fire, but she thought it would be good to have a ready supply. She counted the wooden matches stored in the house. There was a very large supply but she would begin conserving them.

She sorted laboriously through the heavy rusting iron implements in the lean-to. Some of the things she found she could not identify. She found more pots, too large for her to use. She found some tools. She found three large, heavy axes. And half-buried in the dirt floor of the lean-to, she found a knife similar to Crown's own.

She carried one of the axes onto the verandah. It was heavy, but she found that if she was careful she could handle it. Now she could cut wood for fires and not rely only on gathering it.

She sat on the verandah with the knife in her hand, turning it over and over. The blade was spotted and discolored, but its point and edge were sharp. She rose and walked with it to the edge of the clearing and took hold of the thick stem of a plant. The knife blade sliced easily through it.

The next day, she returned to the lean-to and hauled out the four big pots she had found. One by one, she wrestled them to the stream, washed them as best she could, and spent the morning scrubbing and scraping at them with tough leaves and twigs she tore from the thick undergrowth beside the stream.

In the afternoon, she hauled them back and set them down near the steps to the verandah. The pots were deep and wide. They would catch some of the heavy rains.

On each of these days the muscles in her legs and arms and shoulders ached but she felt them growing stronger, felt her appetite grow greater and her sleep at night deeper.

And at last one morning she awoke and opened her eyes and knew that she was going back to the slave tree.

19

It was easier to follow the wedges blazed into the trees than she had thought it would be.

She was stronger now, her legs steadier, her vision sharper, her thoughts clearer. And the vast forest that surrounded her had by now grown to seem less alien and threatening than before.

As she prepared to set out, she recalled the terrible dry thirst she had felt at the tree and she looked around for something to carry water in. The best thing she could find was a large mug with a handle.

She examined the big pots she had set out in front of the house. There was rainwater in the bottom of each. To rid it of floating insects, she filtered some of the water through one of Edwin's shirts, then filled her mug.

It was awkward to carry at first. She spilled some of the water, and sipped a little, but by the time she reached the slave tree the mug was still half full.

The trail of wedges brought her to the clearing at the same spot where they had emerged before. It looked familiar to her but she almost felt that she was seeing it for the first time: the circular open space in the forest, the ring of bright sunlight, and the thick, dark tree at the center.

She looked to her right, toward where the Indians were buried. The ground there had been disturbed, scraped and clawed at by things of the forest, the bodies dug up and dragged a little distance away and devoured. She saw some bones scattered around. The meat was gone from them. What the animals had not torn free had been eaten by insects, consumed by the hungry forest itself.

She scanned the circle of shadow beneath the tree.

She saw three pods lying on the ground where they had recently fallen.

The nearest of them lay between her and the trunk of the tree.

She walked slowly toward it.

She had no idea how much time had passed since it had dropped from its branch. It might have been minutes or hours or days.

She sank to her knees beside it and touched the rough surface of the pod. She ran her fingers along it, then pressed against it with the palm of her hand. It was stiff but she thought it yielded a little beneath the pressure.

She shifted her position and bent to see what she could of the underside. The curving bottom of the pod looked damp and discolored.

She hesitated, looked across to the two other pods on the ground.

Then she slid her hand through the slit she had cut in the side of her dress and grasped the handle of the knife she carried in Edwin's hidden belt.

She pressed her lips together. Quickly, she inserted the knife blade into the seam near the stem end of the pod, as she had seen Crown do. It went in easily and she was at once surprised to find that it sliced quickly along the line of the seam.

On her knees, bracing herself with her left hand on the ground, she moved sideways and easily drew the knife the rest of the pod's length.

She stood, moved around to the other side, bent over and worked her fingers into the seam and pulled the top of the pod back sharply.

It came away so easily that she fell backward.

A foul odor of decay rose like a mist, almost visible, from the pod, a thick, choking, sickening smell that filled the air all around.

She scrambled to her feet, took several quick steps backward, away from the smell.

But she made herself stop and hold her ground. She had to look at what was in the pod. She turned her head to the side, drew in a deep lungful of air, fetid as it was, and held her breath.

She stepped quickly forward and looked over the upright top of the pod and saw what it contained.

She gasped and sucked in more of the thick smell of rotting, decaying matter.

In the pod was the distorted but recognizable outline of a human body. Light-skinned, narrow-eyed. Female. Lying on its back. Head, torso, arms, legs. Henrietta's brain registered the pointed nipples, the smooth mound between the legs. Clearly female. But beginning to decay now. Skin marked with dark blotches. And crawling with insects, throbbing with brown and red and white shiny larvae. The vine-like cord that connected the abdomen to the pod had collapsed and shriveled and lay limp and lifeless across the body.

Henrietta backed away quickly, then turned, ran, finally stopped in the ring of sunlight. She pressed her hands to her face and found she still held the knife.

Gagging and gasping for clean air, she nonetheless reminded herself to be careful with the blade. She must not cut herself.

She breathed deeply. When she felt able, she turned back to the shadowed ground and the tree and slowly walked toward the second of the pods.

Cautiously, she sank to one knee, but this time she did so on the side of the pod away from the seam. She sucked air deep into her lungs, held it, and went to work.

As with the first pod, the blade sank easily into the seam. She pulled it quickly along the line, half the length of the pod, stopped, took hold of the cut edge, pulled hard. The top of the pod bent back toward her, then tore open.

The same choking smell of decay rose up in a cloud.

She saw another glistening figure, this one yellowish, in the same early stage of decay. In that first instant, confused, she thought it lacked a face, lacked defining features, and then she realized that this one was lying in the pod on its front, the face turned toward the side, and she was seeing the back of its head, covered with jet black hair. Then she recognized the buttocks, but they were sinking, collapsing inward.

She rose, turned, bolted away.

This time, she had to fall quickly to her knees, her hands pressed flat on the ground, to keep her head low enough until her brain received enough oxygen and her stomach stopped churning.

When she felt steadier, she sat on the ground in the sun and rested.

She was thirsty. She rose and circled around the edge of the clearing in the sunlight to where she had put down her mug of rainwater. She sipped a little, enough to moisten her mouth and throat and wash away the smell she thought she could taste.

She looked around for the pod and the body she'd seen the last time she was here. She thought she knew the exact spot, but if the thing was there, it had decayed and rotted into the mass of soft vegetation beneath the tree.

She carried the mug back with her as she approached the last remaining pod. She put it down on the ground nearby.

She did what she had done the last time, kneeling on the solid side of the pod and reaching across it to cut at the seam.

She had trouble inserting the point of the blade. She increased the pressure and, with an effort, pushed it in several inches. She resettled her grip on the handle of the knife. Her wrist was at an awkward angle this way but she did not want to do this from the other side. She forced the blade along the seam. The pod resisted and she made only slow progress. She stopped to rest for a few seconds and felt the wide, flat top of the pod with her other hand. She thought it felt strong and firm, like the first one she had seen, that first time at the tree.

It took her a long while and hard work but at last she had cut along the full length of the pod.

She started to replace the knife in the belt beneath her dress but then she thought better of it. She laid the knife on the ground, ready to her hand if it was needed.

She got a grip on the edge of the pod, at the seam, and pulled it back sharply with all the force she could muster. It snapped apart lengthwise. She fell back. Remembered to snatch at the knife.

Another male.

Similar to the first she had seen, with the same connecting cord to the abdomen curving and firm. Its skin was dark but not black, and the facial features made her think of the Indians who had manned the *batelão*.

She stood, stared at the figure, backed away, came close again, knelt and slowly bent forward. There was no smell. She kept the knife in her hand, raised, ready.

It looked alive, dormant, but alive, despite the pale green coating that covered the body, face, everything. The face was turned to the side, the mouth partly open, the pale green fluid seeping from it.

After a very long time, fingers trembling, breath held, she reached out and touched it with her left hand. She touched the chest and it yielded like firm flesh with bone beneath. She touched the abdomen. The neck. Finally, the face.

It felt like flesh. It felt warm. It felt alive. She took hold of the cord to the abdomen with her left hand and raised the knife in her right. But she had to lower it again because the blade was trembling in her hand. She steadied herself, held her breath, released it, tried again.

She cut the cord close to the abdomen.

A drop of green fluid welled up from the stump, but nothing more.

She waited. Nothing happened.

As she stared at the figure, she became aware of her own conviction that it was alive.

And she knew in an ancient and wordless manner what she had to do. Her hands shot out toward the mouth, then instantly withdrew. Fingers moving faster than thought, she used the knife to cut a piece of material from the bottom of her dress.

Now the knife was in her way. In an instant, she had pushed it beneath her dress and, more carefully, slid the naked blade under the belt. She had practiced doing this at the house so as not to slice into her own flesh.

She took hold of the chin, turned it, pushed her fingers and the end of the piece of dress material into the mouth, and wiped out the green fluid. She saw or felt teeth, tongue, palate, thought she heard a faint sigh.

She wiped the green coating away from the nostrils and the eyes, then the ears and the rest of the face.

Hardly thinking, she drew back and looked at it. The face was almost clean now. Did the lips move? The nostrils? Did it breathe?

Empty of thought, she reached for the mug of water, moved it closer to her side.

She dropped the piece of cloth. She dipped her fingers in the water and quickly brought them to the figure's lips, wet the lips, shook the last drops into the partly open mouth. She did it again. And a third time.

And as she touched the lips yet again with her wet fingers, felt their softness, the lips moved and the figure's eyes fluttered and opened. Long eyelashes lifted and unfocused dark eyes stared upward. The head moved of its own will slightly from side to side.

A deep shiver ran all through her, her shoulders twitching with the force of it.

Behind her: a voice.

"It's alive! My God, it's alive!"

She screamed, jumped violently, lost her balance and fell across the figure in front of her, spun around on the ground, scrambled away, eyes wide and shoulders hunched in fright.

Crown stood above her.

20

When she recovered from the fright, she crawled back to the pod and the creature inside it and, heart still pounding, struggled to ignore Crown.

The mug of water had not been spilled and she picked it up and administered more of it, very slowly, to the quivering lips of the black figure. The eyes remained open now, moving all around, unfocused, unseeing, but alive. After a while, when her fingers brought a few drops of water yet again to the smooth lips, the tongue moved and sought the moisture.

She concentrated on what she was doing and did not look at Crown.

He stood over her, circled around her and the pod and the dark figure, paced up and down, looked up and searched among the branches of the tree for more pods that might be ripe enough to fall. He strode away and glanced briefly at the two pods on the ground whose contents were dead and rotting, and then dismissed them from his mind.

Back and back he came to stand over her, breathing heavily and moving impatiently around her.

Kneeling at the other side of the pod, he took hold of the face and twisted it roughly toward him.

"Leave him alone!" Henrietta screamed. "Leave him alone!"

She grabbed at his wrist, his fingers, his hand that held the face, and tried to pull them away.

Crown jerked his hand free of her grip, raised it quickly beside her head, prepared to strike her, but then he hesitated and sat back on his heels. His eyes glared at her but he controlled himself and stood up.

"Get out of the way," he told her, his voice steady, level, frightening. "I'm taking it back to the house."

"No!"

"Get out of the way."

She didn't move.

Crown stepped across the pod, took hold of her shoulder, lifted her, then shoved her away. She fell on her side and lay there, looking up at him.

Crown ignored her.

He straddled the body, bent and placed his hands under the creature's arms, and pulled it up roughly. The greenish coating made it slippery and he lost his grip on it and it tumbled back limply to the ground.

He lifted it again with a better grip, taking hold of one wrist and one ankle, crouched, and hoisted it across his broad shoulders as if it were a deer he had shot.

He did not even glance at Henrietta.

She watched him walk away, silently crossing the clearing. At the far side of it, he stepped from the sunlight into the forest, through the thick undergrowth, and disappeared in the direction of the trail back to the *estância*.

She stood there, breathing hard, chest heaving, for a long time.

But in the end, she walked slowly across the clearing, entered the forest, and followed him back to the house.

21

When she reached the *estância*, she saw from the shadows at the edge of the clearing that the day was almost ended.

Crown had dumped the figure on the verandah at the top of the steps. It lay on its back, but she saw at once that it was moving. She saw random shivers and the faint flexing of muscles. The fingers slowly clenched and opened, clenched together and opened. The feet and toes moved. The head rocked a little from side to side to side. The stump at the abdomen, where she had cut through the cord, was still firm but now it was pushed a little to one side, perhaps from being pressed against Crown's back.

The eyes were open, moving randomly.

Crown stood over it, his hands on his hips.

"Give it more water," he told her. He kept his gaze fixed on the creature at his feet.

She brought water and administered it slowly and steadily.

Once, while there was still light, she rose and, without a word, walked off toward the side of the house to the place in the forest where she customarily relieved herself. When she had done that, she walked directly to the back of the house and entered by the door next to the cooking area. She found her book and her pencil and, ignoring Crown outside, wrote in the book for a couple of minutes, describing the day's events. When she was finished, she put down the dull pencil without reading over what she had written. Then she returned to the verandah.

Crown remained where she had left him, sitting on the steps near the creature. She did not speak to him, nor he to her.

Soon, darkness arrived and swiftly covered the forest and the clearing.

Henrietta fetched two lanterns from inside, lighted them, and hung them from the hooks above the verandah steps. They cast a circle of amber light with the figure, limbs still moving, at the center of it. Its chest rose and fell now in shallow breathing. A low, deep sound, like distant moaning, came from it. In the dim light, it looked even more like the Indians.

Crown paced in silence. Then he sat in one of the rocking chairs on the verandah next to the door, his legs spread apart, his boots near the figure's head. He watched the form, watched her.

Eventually, she could no longer keep her eyes open. She was sitting on the floor of the verandah, her feet on the steps. She lowered herself to the floor and lay sideways.

As she sank helplessly into sleep, she was aware that Crown leaned forward, lifted the pot of water she'd been using, and splashed some of it on the creature's mouth and face. It jerked its head away and blinked its eyes, making a new sound in its throat.

Crown sat back and continued his watch.

Henrietta sank into sleep.

When she opened her eyes, morning light blinded her. She lay unmoving at first, trying to see and to sort out the meaning of what she saw.

The figure had been pulled around to a different position. Its head still moved from side to side but it lay now with its buttocks at the edge of the top step. Crown had placed its feet on a lower step and spread the creature's knees apart.

As Henrietta's vision cleared, she saw Crown just crouching down on the ground, then kneeling on the lowest step, between the figure's knees. She saw him reach for the dark sex that hung before his eyes but she could not comprehend what he was doing.

Then she saw the knife in his hand.

"What . . ?"

Crown looked up at her.

The thought struck her suddenly that he looked hesitant, momentarily confused, unaccustomed as he was to being less than expert at everything he did. And then she saw his intention.

She sat upright.

"No! Don't!"

Crown growled something at her and turned his gaze back to what he was doing.

She pushed herself to her knees beside the prostrate form and threw herself forward.

"No!"

With his left hand, Crown took hold of the scrotum, lifted it and pulled it forward, away from the body. Then he sliced the knife quickly through the stretched soft skin above the globes.

22

The creature howled. The high-pitched shriek went on and on, choked off almost at once, and began again. The face was contorted, the teeth bared, the eyes rolling upward. The body jerked and twitched in violent spasms. It writhed helplessly on its back, unable to rise. It could not get away, could not escape the searing pain. Its limbs were too weak. And there was a rope tied around its neck that had not been there before, the other end affixed to one of the wooden braces beneath the steps.

Crown tossed away the bloody scrotum.

Red blood welled up between the legs, spurted out onto the steps, then spurted again, and again, pooling quickly on one step, staining the dry wood, and running off the edge to the next step below. There was blood on the fingers of Crown's left hand, on the knife, on his right hand, and the blood ran down quickly from step to step and soaked into the knees of his pants where he knelt.

The screaming turned into guttural choking noises, slowly dying away for lack of breath.

Crown stood up.

When Henrietta lunged toward him, she lost her balance and slid down the steps. She was aware of sharp pain flaring hotly in her hip and knee, but she felt it only as if from a distance.

And as she bent and struggled to right herself, she felt yet another pain, a sharp stab, in the fleshy mound just below her belly.

She caught her breath, then slowly, carefully braced her weight on one arm and pushed herself up. The other she kept pressed against her stomach.

Crown was in a rage of frustration and confusion. He roared at the thing that lay gasping and keening now, twitching and bleeding, inexorably, steadily, bleeding to death at his feet. Half incoherent, he sputtered in his fury. His actual words did not register on Henrietta's mind, only his colossal anger that this thing too, like all the others, was going to die and rob him of his harvest.

Henrietta got to her feet.

There was blood everywhere.

The creature had bled red blood, red human blood, not green or white sap. Its flesh was not crisp fibrous material that held only water, but ordinary firm flesh, human flesh.

Flesh that yielded blood, so much blood, that was red and bright. The blood had finally convinced her. That and the scream.

And Crown had killed him. It. Him.

She saw everything now with intense clarity.

There were two things she had to do.

Crown stood on the steps, toeing the figure with his boot to make it react and show some sign of life. It continued weakly spurting blood from between its legs. It twitched a little. It made ragged gasping sounds.

She moved slowly away from Crown, up the steps, doubled over a little, one hand still pressed to her stomach.

Crown ignored her.

She crossed the verandah and walked slowly inside to the table. Her book and her pencil still lay on it. She picked up the pencil stub and, without sitting, rumpled the pages open to where she had last written.

She scribbled "red blood" and "flesh" and "human." Then "Crown" and "castrate" and "kill."

She left the book open on the table and turned toward the door.

She slid her hand through the slit she'd made in her dress and grasped the handle of the knife she'd been holding in place against her stomach. She had forgotten it earlier, only became aware of it again when she fell down the steps and its point stabbed into her and sliced her flesh down there, where the hair was. She was bleeding. She felt the warm stickiness between her legs, blood running slowly on the inside of her thigh.

She went to the door and out onto the verandah. She held the knife hidden at her side in the folds of her dress.

Crown, breathing hard, his face coated with sweat, stared down at the dark shape that lay still now, twisted on the floor of the verandah, its head pulled to one side by the rope around its neck.

As Henrietta came up close to Crown, he drew back his right foot and kicked savagely at the thing's chest. The toe of his boot made a hard thump against the flesh and there was a muffled cracking sound.

And in the instant that Crown was off balance on one foot, Henrietta threw herself forward and plunged the blade of the knife into his neck and in the very second that she felt the impact of her blow she twisted and pushed and dug deep with the blade and made it slice and tear at everything in his neck that resisted.

Crown's eyes flew wide and he staggered but, even so, and even as blood gushed from his throat onto her hand and arm, from long instinct his fingers flew to the gun at his hip and he drew it and cocked it and fired in her direction. She smelled the acrid explosion of gunpowder an instant before the flame erupted in the middle of her body and she twisted the knife once more and felt something in his neck yield to the blade and split apart and she heard coughing as the light faded away to darkness and silence and she sank down and down and then Crown tumbled heavily backwards and lay still as his own blood drained away.

The insects came first and settled on the fresh blood and drank it and then began at the eyes. The birds came. Animals emerged from the forest, entered the clearing, approached the house cautiously at first, tugged warily at the meat, and then tore at it and ate. The sun rose higher and burned even hotter. Rain pounded down at the house and muddied the dirt of the clearing and buried the bones left scattered there. And soon the forest, sensing only stillness in the clearing, began moving forward to reclaim the ground it had lost only briefly in its ageless span of time, its secrets still held deep and silent in its heart.